Noddy and
the Magic Watch

Collins

An Imprint of HarperCollins*Publishers*

NODDY

CLOCKWORK MOUSE

BIG-EARS

MARTH

TESSIE BEAR

GOBBO

MR PLOD

MASTER TUBBY BEAR

ONKEY

SLY

MR WOBBLY MAN

BUMPY DOG

It had been a busy time in Toyland . . .

All week, Noddy had been taking the toys for rides in his car. Now it was time to count up how much money he had made!

"My word, Noddy," gasped Tessie, as he poured all the money on to the table. "You *have* earned a lot of sixpences!"

"As I've worked so hard," Noddy explained, "I shall give myself a present – a watch."

Tessie Bear thought this was a very sensible idea.

Bumpy Dog also seemed to agree. With a wag of his tail, he jumped up, knocking over all the sixpences!

Noddy bought a beautiful watch from Dinah Doll's stall. He thought it was the finest he had ever seen!

On reaching Big-Ears' house, Noddy proudly showed him his new watch. But Big-Ears' reaction was not quite what Noddy had been expecting...

"Oh dear! Oh dear me!" exclaimed Big-Ears, staggering backwards. "That is an ancient Brownie watch!"

Big-Ears immediately consulted his ancient *Book of Brownie Wisdom.*

"This watch can make very strange magic," he said gravely, reading from the huge book. "Never wear this watch on Stony Bridge when it chimes twelve o'clock on a Saturday!"

Noddy became very excited when he heard this. It was Saturday today – and it was very nearly midday! What on earth could this mysterious happening be?

But Big-Ears warned Noddy to keep well away from Stony Bridge, at least until twelve o'clock had passed.

"I promise!" Noddy replied, hearing how solemn Big-Ears' voice was.

Noddy really meant to keep his promise. And he might well have done, if only he hadn't given Martha Monkey a lift and told her all about his magic watch.

"Let's go and find out what happens!" Martha Monkey suggested mischievously.

Noddy told her about Big-Ears' warning, but Martha Monkey told him that he should be more adventurous.

"Er... I suppose you might be right," said Noddy and he swung his car around, heading for Stony Bridge!

"Is it twelve o'clock yet?" Martha Monkey asked excitedly as soon as she and Noddy reached Stony Bridge.

Noddy glanced at his watch.

"Nearly!" he replied nervously – there was only one minute to go!

The watch started to chime twelve o'clock. Noddy was breathless with excitement. But nothing mysterious seemed to happen at all!

"What happened? Did you see anything, Martha?" he asked, very puzzled.

But Martha could not reply. She was frozen. She could not move a muscle. She could not even blink.

The stream had stopped flowing too. Nothing moved. Not even Noddy's car!

Very worried, Noddy ran all the way back to Toy Town.

"Mr Plod, can you help me please?" he panted anxiously. "Martha Monkey is stuck!"

But to Noddy's horror, he saw that Mr Plod was frozen as well!

And so was Bert Monkey, and Mr Tubby Bear, and the Skittle children!

Every single toy was frozen!

Noddy was very upset. He knew it was all his fault!!

Noddy hurried to Big-Ears' house, certain that he would not have been affected by the strange magic.

"Oh, he is stuck as well!" he gasped.

Big-Ears was sitting quite still in his chair, a glass of lemonade halfway to his lips!

As poor Noddy wondered what to do, he noticed
Big-Ears' ancient *Book of Brownie Wisdom* on the table.
It was open at the very page which described how to
undo the strange magic.

"Place four magic things on Stony Bridge..." Noddy
read slowly. "Something that's round and a thing with a
spot. A thing that's got spikes and something that's not!"

Noddy rushed out of Big-Ears' house in search of the four special things. He had to hurry because the *Book of Brownie Wisdom* said that the magic could only be undone if all four things were collected within the hour.

Luckily, he found one of the things almost at once.

"You're a thing with a spot!" he cried, picking up a ladybird.

Soon Noddy found the next special thing.

"Something that's round!" he cried with delight as he passed a frozen Bumpy Dog jumping up at a frozen ball.

By the time Noddy reached the café, there were only fifteen minutes left to undo the magic.

By a stroke of luck, he found the third special thing just moments later.

"A thing that's got spikes!" he exclaimed as he spotted Miss Pink Cat, quite silent for once, with her fork in mid-air.

Noddy searched high and low for the last thing he needed.

"Something that's not?" he muttered to himself, puzzled.

Suddenly, he realised the magic book meant a knot! And that's exactly what he spotted in Dinah Doll's raised frozen hand – a scarf with a knot!

Glancing at his watch, Noddy was dismayed to find that time was running out.

"Five minutes to reach Stony Bridge!" he cried.

Noddy ran as fast as he could past all his frozen friends.
He ran past a frozen Clockwork Clown.

He hardly noticed a frozen Jumbo because he was so worried about getting to Stony Bridge on time.

With only seconds to go, Noddy stepped on to
Stony Bridge.

"Just a few seconds left!" he gasped to Martha
Monkey, who was still frozen above the ground exactly
where he left her.

Carefully, Noddy laid the four special things on the ground.

He had scarcely finished when his watch began to chime one o'clock.

Was the magic going to work?

To Noddy's immense relief, the magic did start to work. All of a sudden, Martha Monkey was moving and talking again.

But Martha did not know that she had been frozen still for the last hour. Noddy's watch once again read twelve o'clock. It was as if nothing had happened at all.

"Noddy, your silly watch isn't magic," she said crossly, "because nothing mysterious has happened!"

Toys were starting to walk and talk again all over Toyland.

Dinah Doll was very puzzled. She wondered where the scarf that she had been about to sell to Sammy Sailor had disappeared to.

Noddy had borrowed it, of course, while Dinah had been frozen by the magic!

Noddy had borrowed Miss Pink Cat's fork as well, and it was only now that she noticed it was missing.

   As she started to eat again, she accidentally put her nice clean paw into the sticky cake and cried out in dismay, "Agh! Where is my fork?"

Noddy was very relieved that no one in Toy Town realised they had been frozen for the last hour.

He was especially glad that Big-Ears had not guessed. His dear friend would certainly have been very cross with him otherwise!

Noddy decided it was time to return the four things he
had secretly borrowed.

The last thing he returned was Bumpy Dog's ball. As
Bumpy Dog jumped up for the ball, he nearly knocked
Noddy to the ground.

Far from being cross, Noddy simply laughed. He surely
deserved a lot worse after all the trouble he had caused.

He decided there and then never to meddle in magic
again – and always to listen to Big-Ears' advice!

This edition first published in Great Britain by HarperCollins Publishers Ltd in 2000

3 5 7 9 10 8 6 4 2

ISBN: 0 00 136173 2

Reproduction by Graphic Studio S.r.l. Verona
Printed in Italy by Garzanti Verga S.r.l.

MORE NODDY BOOKS FOR YOU TO ENJOY

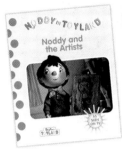

Noddy and the Artists

Noddy and the Bouncing Ball

Noddy is Caught in a Storm

Noddy and the Driving Lesson

Noddy is Far Too Busy

Noddy and the Goblins

Noddy and the Noisy Drum

Noddy the Nurse

Noddy and the Singing Bush

Noddy Tells a Story

Noddy Tidies Toyland

Noddy and the Treasure Map